PRICE STERN SLOAN
Published by the Penguin Group
Penguin Group (USA) Inc., 375 Hudson Street, New York, New York 10014, USA
Penguin Group (Canada), 90 Eglinton Avenue East, Suite 700, Toronto, Ontario M4P 2Y3, Canada
(a division of Pearson Penguin Canada Inc.)
Penguin Books Ltd., 80 Strand, London WC2R ORL, England
Penguin Group Ireland, 25 St. Stephen's Green, Dublin 2, Ireland
(a division of Penguin Books Ltd.)
Penguin Group (Australia), 250 Camberwell Road, Camberwell, Victoria 3124, Australia
(a division of Pearson Australia Group Pty. Ltd.)
Penguin Books India Pvt. Ltd., 11 Community Centre, Panchsheel Park, New Delhi—110 017, India
Penguin Group (NZ), 67 Apollo Drive, Rosedale, North Shore 0632, New Zealand
(a division of Pearson New Zealand Ltd.)
Penguin Books (South Africa) (Pty.) Ltd., 24 Sturdee Avenue,
Rosebank, Johannesburg 2196, South Africa

Penguin Books Ltd., Registered Offices: 80 Strand, London WC2R ORL, England

Library of Congress Cataloging-in-Publication Data is available.

ISBN 978-0-8431-9948-2   10 9 8 7 6 5 4 3 2 1

DREAMWORKS®
SHReK
FOREVER AFTER™

THE MOVIE STORYBOOK

BY CATHY HAPKA
ILLUSTRATED BY LARRY NAVARRO

Once upon a time there was an ogre named Shrek. He was famous throughout Far Far Away for rescuing Princess Fiona with true love's kiss. Now they were living happily ever after. Or were they?

Things were very different for Shrek and Fiona now. Tour buses came from far and wide to catch a glimpse of the famous ogre. Plus, Shrek and Fiona had three babies—Fergus, Farkle, and Felicia—who were growing bigger every day. Bigger ogre babies meant bigger noises, bigger burps, bigger smells...and more work. Shrek never had time to enjoy a nice mud bath anymore. It felt as if he barely had time to be an ogre!

We ♥ Shrek

★ Star Tours Chariot ★

Before Shrek knew it, the babies were turning one. Fiona threw a big party, but Shrek wasn't having any fun—and it only got worse when the guests begged him to do his famous roar.

Finally, Fiona told Shrek to get the ogre-shaped birthday cake. "Isn't it cute?" someone said. But Shrek didn't like it. Ogres weren't supposed to be cute!

He'd had enough. *WHAM!* Shrek slammed his fist into the cute cake and stormed out of the party.

Rumpelstiltskin was a scheming deal-maker who longed to rule Far Far Away. He watched Shrek at the birthday party and came up with a plan.

Rumpel invited Shrek into his carriage and offered him a magical deal called "Ogre for a Day." People would be afraid of Shrek again. He could do whatever he wanted.

And all Rumpel wanted in return? "A day," he said. "One you wouldn't even remember. Like a day when you were a baby."

That sounded pretty good to Shrek. He signed the magical contract. "Have a nice day!" Rumpel laughed as he and his carriage vanished.

Shrek sat on the ground with Rumpel's contract in his hand. Nothing seemed different.

Then Shrek turned to see a bunch of people running away from him.

"Ogre!" they cried in terror.

He laughed with delight. This was more like it!

Shrek started scaring people left and right. He had a great time! Especially when he saw an "Ogre Wanted" poster with his face on it.

"Sure is great to be wanted again!" he said happily.

WANTED

OGRES
REWARD

Shrek raced home to the swamp to see his family. That's when the fun stopped. There was no sign of his house, his kids, his friends... or Fiona.

Uh-oh. This wasn't what he'd signed up for! What had he done?

Suddenly, a squadron of witches came flying over the swamp. They were on ogre patrol!

Shrek fought back. But there were too many witches. They took him captive and locked him in a carriage.

Shrek heard singing outside the carriage. Familiar singing.

"Donkey, what's happening?" he grumbled. Then his eyes snapped open. Donkey was pulling the cart!

"Look, ogre," Donkey said. "You must have me confused with some other talking donkey. How do you know my name, anyway?"

Shrek couldn't believe his best friend didn't recognize him. But he figured out why as the witches took him toward Rumpelstiltskin's castle. Rumpel had tricked him—and taken over Far Far Away! Now the whole kingdom was run-down and miserable.

"Don't worry, Donkey," Shrek said. "I'll get us our lives back."

Donkey rolled his eyes. "Put a little mustard on mine, Captain Crazy."

Inside the castle, Rumpel greeted Shrek with a laugh. "There you are. The guy that made all this possible."

Then he explained that Shrek had signed over a day from his past. And not just any day—the day he was born!

That meant Shrek had never existed at all in Rumpel's world. He'd never rescued Fiona. Instead, the king and queen had signed over the kingdom to Rumpel in exchange for their daughter's freedom.

"But you haven't heard the best part," Rumpel finished with a cackle. "Since you were never born, once this day comes to an end, so will you!"

Shrek couldn't believe what Rumpel had told him about the Ogre for a Day contract. He had to fix this!

Desperately, Shrek broke free, grabbed Donkey, and fought his way out of the castle on a witch's broom. Once they were safe in the woods, Shrek convinced Donkey that he wasn't going to hurt him. That's when Donkey told Shrek that all of Rumpel's contracts had an exit clause. Shrek soon found it: "true love's kiss." Shrek was elated.

"If Fiona and I share true love's kiss, everything will go back to the way it was before I ever made this deal. I can get my life back!" he cried.

Shrek couldn't wait to find Fiona.

Donkey and Shrek looked for Fiona but couldn't find her. Then Donkey got distracted by a stack of waffles.

"Don't eat that!" Shrek warned.

Too late. When Donkey licked the waffles, he fell into a trap! Shrek leaped down after his friend and found a secret camp full of other ogres.

"Suit up, greenie!" one ogre barked. "Welcome to the resistance."

Shrek was stunned. First he stopped the other ogres from cooking Donkey for dinner. Then he met the leader of the ogre army camp. It was Fiona!

Shrek was thrilled to see Fiona. If he could get her to kiss him, they could go back to their real lives!

But Fiona had no idea who Shrek was, and she didn't care. She was busy planning an attack on Rumpel's forces to free Far Far Away from his evil rule.

"Puss?" Shrek said in amazement when he sneaked into Fiona's tent.

He could hardly believe it. Tough, brave Puss In Boots was now bootless Puss the pampered pet!

Later, Fiona wasn't happy to find Shrek in her tent. She was even less happy when he tried to kiss her. So she kicked him out. Shrek needed a new plan...

Before the attack on Rumpel's forces, Shrek told Fiona about the happy life they shared in the real world. And Fiona almost believed him. Then Fiona started to dance with him.

"I can't control myself!" she cried.

It was the Pied Piper. Rumpel had hired him to capture the ogres with magical music, forcing the ogres to dance... right into Rumpel's dungeon!

"We must get them away from the music!" Puss cried. He and Donkey galloped in and grabbed the dancing couple.

"Puss and Donkey to the rescue!" Donkey said. "Hey, I kind of like the sound of that."

While Shrek and Fiona got away, Rumpel captured the rest of the ogres. Desperate to change things, Fiona finally agreed to kiss Shrek. But nothing happened. So Fiona raced away to try to help the other ogres . . . and ended up getting captured herself.

Finally, Shrek realized that he may never get his old life back. So he decided to help Fiona and her ogre army. That way, at least she could be happy.

Shrek went to Rumpel and made his own deal. If Rumpel released all the ogres, Shrek would turn himself in.

But when Rumpel threw Shrek in the dungeon, Fiona was there. "We had a deal!" Shrek yelled at Rumpel. "You agreed to free all ogres!"

"But Fiona isn't all ogre," Rumpel pointed out.

It was true. Since Shrek had never rescued her with true love's kiss, she was still under her curse. She was still part human.

Fiona smiled at Shrek, realizing what he had done just to save her.

That night, Rumpel and his witches threw a party to celebrate their victory over Shrek.

But Puss and Donkey came to the rescue again. They sneaked the ogre army into the palace inside Rumpel's new disco ball. After it was delivered, they all burst out and attacked Rumpel and his witches! Shrek and Fiona worked side by side throughout the heated battle.

Finally, they captured Rumpel.

"Victory is ours!" Fiona cried.

After the battle, Shrek and Fiona shared a happy moment together. "We make a good team," Fiona said with a smile.

"You have no idea," Shrek replied.

Then he looked down and saw his fingers beginning to fade away. His day was up!

"There has to be something we can do!" Fiona cried. She had seen how brave and special Shrek was. And it was at that moment she realized she had fallen in love with him. But was it too late?

Fiona kissed Shrek just as he and the rest of Rumpel's world disappeared.

It worked! True love's kiss had broken Rumpel's contract. Suddenly
Shrek found himself exactly where he wanted to be—back at the ogre babies'
birthday party. Back in his busy, crazy, wonderful old life with Fiona.

And this time he knew he would never take any of it for granted again.
From now on, he would truly enjoy living happily forever after.